This book belongs to...

Why?

An original concept by author Billy Dunne

© Billy Dunne

Illustrated by Rhys Jefferys

MAVERICK ARTS PUBLISHING LTD
Studio 11, City Business Centre, 6 Brighton Road, Horsham,
West Sussex, RH13 5BB, +44 (0)1403 256941

First Published in the UK in 2020 by **MAVERICK ARTS PUBLISHING LTD**

American edition published in 2020 by Maverick Arts Publishing, distributed in the
United States and Canada by Lerner Publishing Group Inc., 241 First Avenue North,
Minneapolis, MN 55401 USA

ISBN 978-1-84886-648-5

www.maverickbooks.co.uk

distributed by Lerner

$$\left(v_{ph}^2 \nabla^2 - \frac{\partial^2}{\partial t^2} \right) E = 0$$

$$\left(v_{ph}^2 \nabla^2 - \frac{\partial^{2'}}{\partial t^2} \right) B = 0$$

$$\nabla \cdot E = 0$$
$$\nabla \times E = -\frac{\partial B}{\partial t}$$
$$\nabla \cdot B = 0$$
$$\nabla \times B = \mu_0 \varepsilon_0 \frac{\partial E}{\partial t}$$

Why?

By **Billy Dunne**

Ilustrated by **Rhys Jefferys**

"What a lovely day!" said Dad,
a **rainbow** overhead.
"You get them when the rain has passed,
and sunshine comes instead."

His daughter stared with wonder at the **rainbow** in the sky.
She looked her daddy in the eyes, and softly asked him, **"Why?"**

"The **colors** in a beam of light are jumbled up together, but **split** apart when passing through a spot of rainy weather."

Red
Orange
Yellow
Green
Blue
Indigo
Violet

Her dad was rather pleased with that,
and started walking by.

Until his daughter made him stop,
by simply asking, **"Why?"**

Beam of light

"When light encounters water,
from the rain that came before.
The **red** light bends a little bit,
the **blue** a little more."

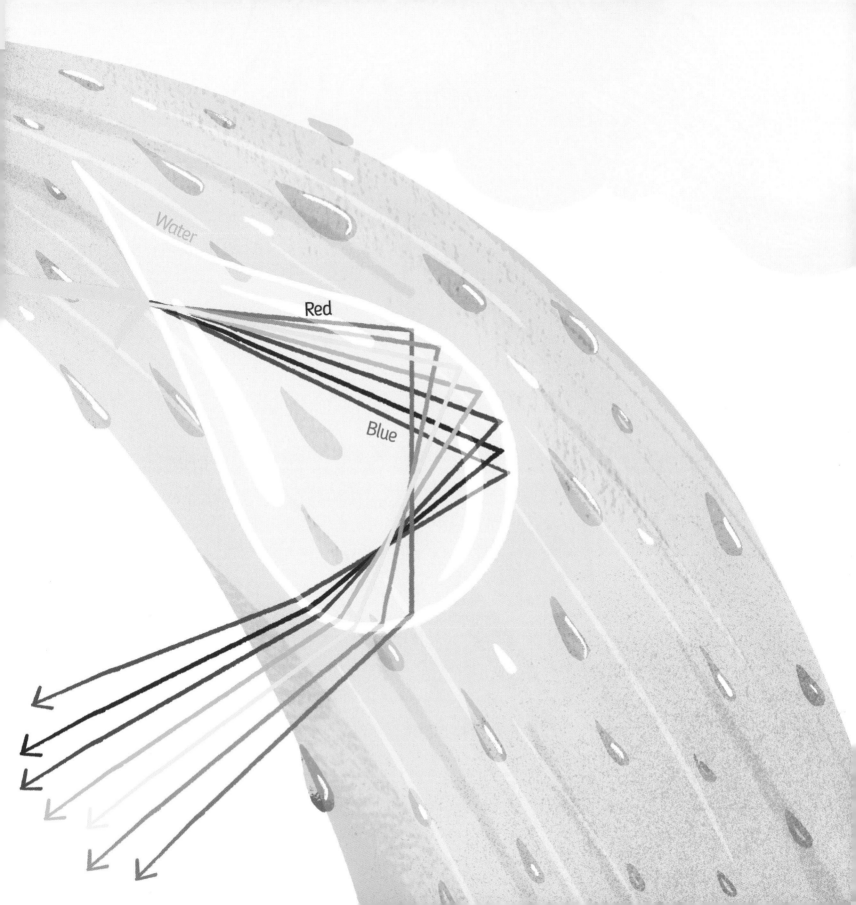

Her daddy eyed her nervously, awaiting her reply.

His darling daughter clapped her hands,
intently asking, **"Why?"**

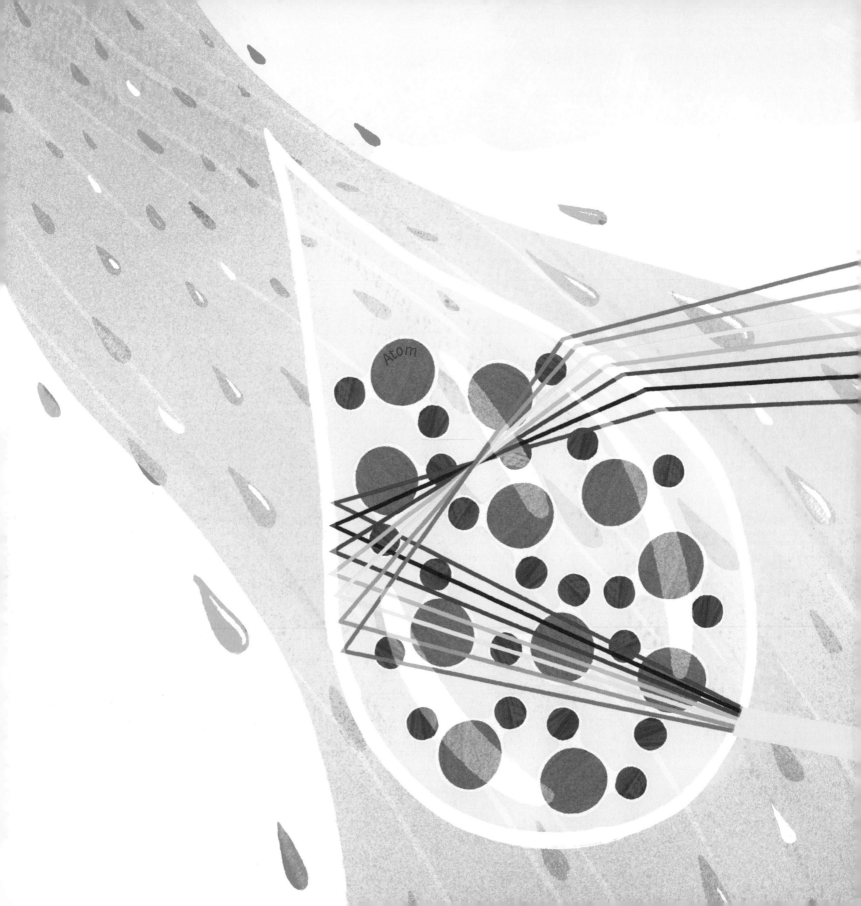

"Well, water's made of **atoms** which are bunched up rather tightly. It really **slows** the blue light down; the red light, only slightly."

Red

Blue

Beam of light

Her daddy wiped his sweating head,
she looked him in the eye.

With growing passion in her voice,
she asked intently, **"Why?"**

"The index of **refraction** of the water when it's bright,

Red

Orange

Yellow

Green

depends upon the **wavelength** of the color of the light."

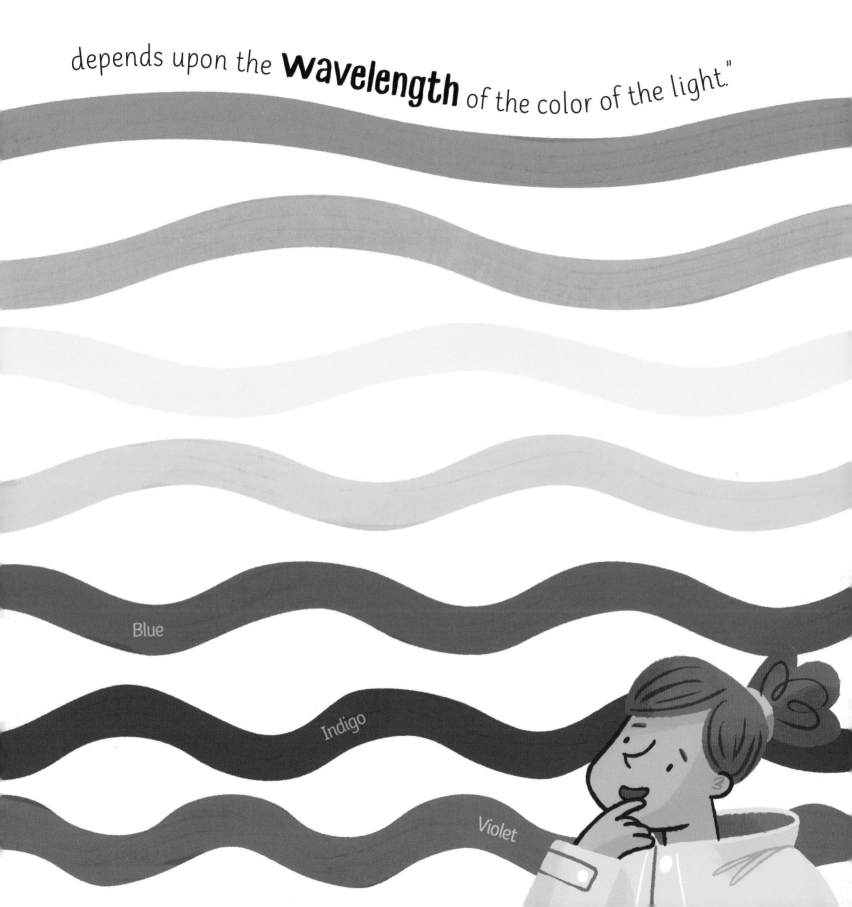

Blue

Indigo

Violet

Collapsing in a nervous heap,
and trying not to cry,
her anxious daddy rocked himself.
His daughter pressed him, **"Why?"**

"The complex **composition** of the photon quantum field, describes the interaction that the **rainbow** has revealed."

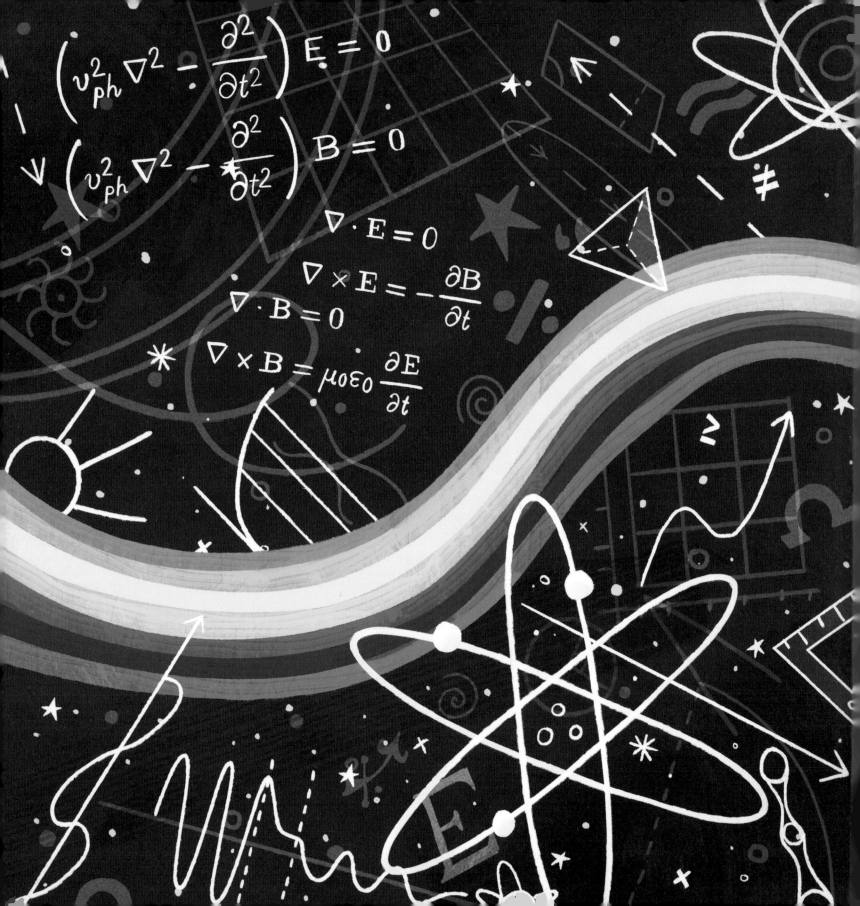

She crawled beside her sobbing Dad,
her hand upon his head.
And whispered with a loving voice,
"You could have...

...simply said."